The PINK REFRIGERATOR

Tim Egan

HOUGHTON MIFFLIN COMPANY
BOSTON 2007

To Ann and the boys
—T. E.

www.houghtonmifflinbooks.com

The text of this book is set in LoType.
The illustrations are ink and watercolor on paper.

Library of Congress Cataloging-in-Publication Data
Egan, Tim.
The pink refrigerator / written and illustrated by Tim Egan.
        p. cm.
Summary: Dodsworth does as little work as he can, collecting items from a junkyard
and placing them in his thrift store for sale, until he happens upon a pink refrigerator
that spurs him to do much more with his life.
ISBN-13: 978-0-618-63154-4 (hardcover)
ISBN-10: 0-618-63154-2 (hardcover)
 [1. Self-actualization—Fiction. 2. Laziness—Fiction.] I. Title.
PZ7.E2815Pin 2007   [Fic]—dc22   2006009816

Printed in Singapore
TWP 10 9 8 7 6 5 4 3 2 1

DODSWORTH LOVED TO DO NOTHING. Now, this isn't to say that he never did anything, because he did. But his motto was basically "Try to do as little as possible."

True, he did get up early each morning and ride to the junkyard. He'd find things that were still useful, like picture frames and dishes, and he'd bring them to his little thrift shop and he'd dust them off and put them on the shelves.

He never sold much, but a little more than enough to get by.

He'd spend the rest of the morning watching his favorite shows,
and at about noon he'd have a bit of cheese and take a long nap.
He'd have dinner at five, and then he'd close the shop, watch a few
more shows, and fall asleep in his chair.

And that was it. That was the life of Dodsworth.

One Sunday morning, Dodsworth spotted an old refrigerator in the junkyard. It was pink and rusty and he walked right past it at first. Then he noticed a magnet on the front. It was a shiny brass globe and it was holding a small piece of paper.

"Nice magnet," he said. He tried to pull it off, but it was stuck.

He pulled harder. "Hmm," he said, "must be rusted on." He got out

his crowbar and used every ounce of energy he had, but the magnet

didn't budge.

Dodsworth looked closer at the note. It seemed too faded to read
at first, but as he focused his eyes, he could just make out two words:
"Make pictures."

Out of curiosity, he opened the refrigerator door, and on the shelves was a beautiful assortment of paints and brushes and a little red sketchbook.

"Well, whaddya know," he said. "These should be worth something." He took them back to the store and placed them in the front window.

Later that morning, a lady came into the store and asked,

"How much is that sketchbook in the window?"

"Oh, I don't know," said Dodsworth. "Five bucks, I guess."

As the lady shuffled through her purse, Dodsworth glanced over at the sketchbook. "Actually," he blurted out, "that sketchbook's not for sale. My mistake."

"Oh, well," said the lady. "Thanks anyway."

After the lady left, Dodsworth picked up the sketchbook.

"Don't know why I did that," he said. "I haven't painted in years."

But that afternoon, he made a picture. It was of the ocean, and even though he'd never actually seen an ocean in real life, it turned out pretty good.

The next morning in the junkyard, he was passing by the refrigerator and, just for the heck of it, he pulled on the magnet. No go.

He leaned in again to read the note. As the words slowly became visible, Dodsworth was astonished. The note now said, "Read more."

"Whoa!" he shouted. "It's a different note. How is that possible?"

He tried to move the magnet again, but it was still stuck.

He opened the door and saw that a whole volume of literary classics filled the shelves.

"These things are worth a fortune!" he said. "I don't know what's happening here, but, wow, what a great refrigerator!"

He quickly went back to the shop and put the books in the window.

A few minutes later, a fellow came by and asked, "Pardon me,
sir, how much for the classic books in your display?"

"Oh," said Dodsworth, "let me think. They're quite rare."

He hesitated. He looked at the books.

"Actually, they've been sold already," he said. "Sorry."

"Ah, well!" said the fellow. "My loss. Good day."

The fellow left and Dodsworth took the books and sat down and started paging through them. They were filled with incredible stories. His favorite one was about a ship that sailed the seven seas. He read for the rest of the day and late into the night until he finally fell asleep.

He woke up really early the next morning and rode over to the junkyard. This time the note said, "Play music." Again, Dodsworth couldn't believe it.

"This is the most amazing refrigerator in history," he whispered. He opened the door, and a shiny brass trumpet was sitting on the shelf.

Dodsworth went back to the shop, but this time he didn't even put the trumpet in the window. He just started playing. Since he didn't know how to play, it didn't sound very good at first, but by nightfall he was able to get a couple of good notes out.

Dodsworth raced to the refrigerator the next morning. This time the note said, "Learn to cook." Inside there was a cookbook and a whole assortment of ingredients.

He rode back to the shop and cooked all day and made one of the best meals he'd ever tasted. He was a gifted chef and he'd never even known it.

The next day, the note said, "Plant a garden," and inside was a tiny little tree and packets of seeds and little shovels and clippers.

Bursting with new enthusiasm, Dodsworth went back and planted all afternoon. He had such a great time that he couldn't believe he hadn't ever done it before.

On Friday morning, Dodsworth rode confidently toward the refrigerator, eager to see what it had to offer. He leaned down and slowly read the note. It said, "Keep exploring."

He opened the door, hoping to find something fabulous, but there was nothing there.

"Hey!" he shouted. "What's going on?" He looked through all the drawers and in the freezer, but the refrigerator was empty.

"That's not fair," he said. "Now you're nothing but an old broken refrigerator."

Disappointed, he slammed the door.

The magnet fell to the ground and the note blew away.

"No!" shouted Dodsworth as he ran through the junkyard,

trying to catch the paper. But a breeze pushed the note

over the fence and up into the sky until it disappeared.

Dodsworth was stunned. His shoulders dropped. "I can't
believe it," he said. "All my good fortune, gone, just like that.
Just when everything was getting started."

He took the magnet back to his shop, sat down, and started
watching his shows again, all the while thinking about what the
note said: "Keep exploring."

At seven-fifteen that night, in the middle of his favorite show, Dodsworth looked at the magnet. He suddenly felt a great sense of wonder about everything. He jumped out of his chair and filled his bicycle with all the things from the refrigerator: the paints and brushes, the sketchbook, the classic books, the trumpet, the cookbook, even the garden.

He walked outside and, using the magnet, he hung a small sign on the door that read, "Went to find an ocean."

He rode to the junkyard and over to the refrigerator.

In the glow of the moon, it looked old and rusty and beautiful.

Dodsworth smiled, tipped his hat, and pedaled down the street.